Lucy

Written and illustrated by Sally O. Lee

Special thanks go to my editor, Victoria Zackheim,
for her editorial and creative talents.

I would also like to thank Stephanie Robinson, Stella French,
and the staff at BookSurge for their encouragement in helping
me to write and illustrate these books.

Finally, I would like to thank my family and friends
for their love and support.

This book is typeset in Palatino.

www.leepublishing.net

To: Mom and Dad

One day, a quiet little bunny named Lucy was playing with her friends and realized that she could not hear in one ear.

One of her friends asked her, "May I see your paintbrush? I've always wanted to learn how to paint," but Lucy didn't answer.

Lucy loved to paint. She rarely went anywhere without a
paintbrush or pencil. Her friend moved closer and asked again,
but this time in a much louder voice.

This made Lucy angry.

"You don't have to yell!" she said,
and then she started to cry. She was
tired of people yelling at her.

Lucy went home and told her mother
what had happened.

"Mom, I can't hear in my left ear. What do you think is wrong?"

"I don't know, dear," said her mother. "Let's go to see
the doctor and tell him about it."
"Okay" said Lucy. "Perhaps he'll know what is wrong."

Lucy and her mother hopped into their car
and off they went.

When they got to the doctor's office, they sat in the
waiting room and waited patiently.

The doctor was very careful when he examined Lucy's ears.

"No carrots in your ears," he said, and
he winked at Lucy's mother.

After the tests were finished, the doctor said,
"Lucy, sometimes little bunnies catch a bad cold or get a virus.
When this happens, it might affect their ears.
It looks like you might be one of those bunnies."

"What does that mean?" asked Lucy.

"It means that you will probably never be able to hear in that ear."

Lucy looked at her mother and then looked at the doctor.

"I know this is sad news," said the doctor. "But I also have
good news. Your other ear is fine, and you will probably always
be able to hear in that ear. And if you notice a change,
you can come back and I'll check your ears again."

"Can I still play with my friends?" asked Lucy.
"Can I paint and draw?
Can I go skating and dancing whenever I want?"

"Of course!" said the doctor with a big smile.
"You can do everything just as before, only now you have
to be a little more careful. You'll need to pay more attention
to the things around you, like people and cars and other things."

Lucy nodded. "What happens if, someday, I can't hear at all?"
Her voice quivered a little.

The doctor put his hand on Lucy's arm and smiled.
"Let's not worry about that now," he said. "If and
when that day arrives, we'll talk about it."

The doctor gave Lucy a big swirly lollipop and helped
her climb down from the examination table.

Lucy was feeling pretty sad. Even though she still had one ear that
could hear just fine, she felt different and alone.

That afternoon, Lucy's father took her for
ice cream and then for a long drive.
They talked about her favorite flavor of ice cream,
which was chocolate, and about the bright green grass,
the blue sky, and the birds on the telephone wires.
They also talked about her ear and how
she couldn't hear out of it..

"I know what you mean, Lucy," said her father.
"We always feel strange when there's something special about us.
As you remember, I have never been able to see
in my right eye."

"Oh, yeah, I forgot that, Dad." replied Lucy.

Her father smiled. "And just think," he said. "You're
the only bunny in your class who can't hear out of one ear.
That makes you special!"

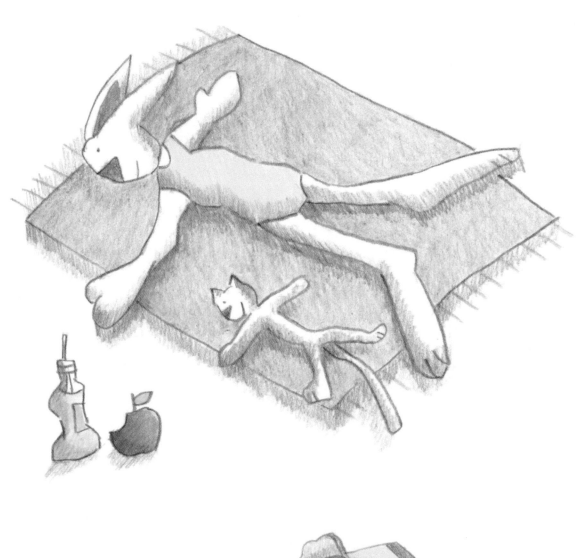

The next day, Lucy went to the beach with her cat, Seymour.
She thought about what her father had said.

"Other kids live with all kinds of problems," she told Seymour.
"Billy, a boy in my class, can't see the words on
the blackboard very well, and Molly reads all the words
backwards when we have our storybook session.

Seymour snuggled very close and licked Lucy's face with
his rough tongue. "Seymour, maybe I am special!"

They went home and Lucy's mother gave her a
big glass of milk and two
chocolate chip cookies. After the snack,
Lucy and Seymour opened the
chest filled with wonderful costumes.
"Let's pretend we're going to a
masquerade ball," she told Seymour
"And maybe someday, Seymour, we will
go to a real masquerade ball!"

Lucy dug through all the costumes and found a
beautiful red velvet dress.
Red was one of her favorite colors. She found
a little red dress for Seymour, too.

The afternoon was filled with....

drawing...

dancing...

and singing!

At the end of the day, Lucy's friends
stopped by her house, and they all
went outside to play.

They ran and laughed and
hopped about, and Lucy understood
that her friends loved her just as she was.

CPSIA information can be obtained at www.ICGtesting.com
Printed in the USA
BVIW12n0420200418
513931BV00015B/32

* 9 7 8 1 5 9 1 0 9 5 6 4 4 *